More Animaniacs Adventures

Two Wacky Tales in One Cool Book!

Adapted by Ellen Stamper
Based upon television scripts by Paul Rugg

Illustrated by Animated Arts
Cover illustration by Allen Helbig

SCHOLASTIC INC.
New York Toronto London Auckland Sydney

ISBN 0-590-53530-7

12 11 10 9 8 7 6 5 4 3 2 1   5 6 7 8 9/9 0/0

Printed in the U.S.A.   23

First Scholastic printing, December 1995

Designed by Alfred Giuliani

Wacky Tale # 1

Temporary Insanity

"*Aaachooo!*" sneezed Miss Fyngolden, secretary to the very important Mr. Thaddeus Plotz, chairman of Warner Bros. Studios. The force of her sneeze sent her desk sailing across the room. As she dragged the desk back to its spot, she pushed the intercom button. "Mr. Plotz, I'm sick, sir," she said. "I'm going home."

Mr. Plotz was not used to having his day interrupted. "You can't be sick!" he shrieked. "There are files to be filed, calls to be called, and typing to be typed. Who will do all my little executive things? Who will make me look important?"

Miss Fyngolden handed him a phone number. "Call this temp agency," she said. "They'll send someone right over."

Grabbing the paper, Mr. Plotz looked confused. "Call them? On the phone?" he asked. "With those little numbers and those buttons?"

"*Aaachoo!*" Miss Fyngolden sneezed again. This time she blew Mr. Plotz onto a coatrack. "I'm sorry, sir. Good-bye, sir," she sniffled, and slammed the door behind her. Mr. Plotz struggled to free himself, but all he could do was hop the coatrack back into his office.

When he had finally wrestled it to the floor and ripped it out of his suit, he collapsed at his desk. "What a relief," he said. But there was no relief in sight. Instead, rows and rows of telephone buttons stared him in the face.

"So I press this *five*? Is that it?" he muttered, pushing a button on the phone. "I can't do this by myself," he whined.

Mr. Plotz hit every button as hard as he could. At last he heard a ring at the other end.

"I did it!" he wept with joy.

He hugged the telephone and jumped up and down.

"Hellooo, Nurse! Can I help you?" a voice said through the phone.

"This is the chief executive officer of Warner Bros.," Mr. Plotz answered. "My secretary's sick and I need help over here . . . who is this?"

"It's me, Yakko!" came the voice. "Don't worry about a thing, T.P. We'll be right over."

Mr. Plotz froze. A look of panic spread over his face. How could this have happened? "Stay away from me, do you hear?" he said into the phone.

The thought of the Animaniacs coming to his office gave Mr. Plotz a colossal headache. He yanked open his desk drawer to get some aspirin. But out popped Yakko, Wakko, and Dot.

"Reporting for work, sir!" Yakko cried, giving his boss a big smooch.

Wakko and Dot jumped on the desk and began to straighten Mr. Plotz's papers and pens.

"Get back to your tower!" Mr. Plotz yelled.

"I thought you needed us to be your sceclataries," Wakko said, shaking salt onto a paperweight and popping it into his mouth.

"You? My sceclataries ... er, secretaries?"
Mr. Plotz corrected himself. "Never!"

RING, RING!

"The phone!" yelled Mr. Plotz in a panic.
He raced to answer it, but his secretary's
phone had even more buttons than his.
"Hello? Hello?" he shouted, punching
button after button.

Yakko, Wakko, and Dot watched
patiently from the desk. Just then the
phone rang again. "I'll get it," they cried,
all diving for the phone at once.

"Look! It's Wayne Newton," Dot said,
pointing across the room. As her brothers
looked away, Dot grabbed the phone from
Mr. Plotz. "Mr. Plotz's office. May I help
you?" Dot asked in her most professional
voice.

Wakko crossed his arms and pouted. "I
never get to get it," he said.

Dot flipped through Mr. Plotz's appointment book. "Yes, Mr. Costner, Thursday at two would be fine. Uh-huh. Okey-dokey. Oh, isn't that sweet. You, too. Buh-bye," she said sweetly, hanging up the phone.

Mr. Plotz looked surprised. Dot had sounded professional, even responsible. "Well . . . ," he said. "I guess it wouldn't hurt for you to stay the day . . . to help me out."

Yakko grabbed Mr. Plotz and shook him up and down. "You'll never live to regret this," he assured him.

Mr. Plotz gave Yakko an uneasy smile.
A short while later Dot sat at Miss
Fyngolden's desk, telephone in hand.

Several calls were already on hold as Dot pushed a button. "Still holding, Mr. Schwarzenegger? Oh, I'd love the recipe. Stay on the line," she chirped, punching another button. "Still there, Mr. Eastwood? Keep holding." Dot pressed yet another button. "Miss Pfeiffer, keep holding."

"How come you keep putting everybody on hold?" Wakko asked.

"Cuz Mr. Plotz is very busy, Wakko," Dot replied.

In his office, Mr. Plotz sat tapping his fingers on his desk. He had absolutely nothing to do. "My heavens, it's a slow day," he said aloud. "I wonder why I haven't gotten any calls."

He was about to take a sip of coffee when there was a knock on the door. "Come in," he said.

"Hello!" Yakko screeched, popping out of Mr. Plotz's coffee cup!

"Don't do that!" yelled Mr. Plotz.

"I'm sorry, T.P., but these things need your signature," Yakko said, holding up a big stack of papers.

Mr. Plotz clapped his hands and began to smile. "Oh goody. I like writing my name," he said.

"Sign here," Yakko ordered. He yanked a pen out of Mr. Plotz's ear and placed paper after paper in front of him.

In the middle of signing his name to one paper, Mr. Plotz looked up at Yakko. "By the way," he asked, "what am I signing?"

"Oh, well, you know. A little of that. A little of this," Yakko replied. He smiled happily. Mr. Plotz had just signed a check made out to Yakko Warner for $80 zillion dollars!

Back in the outer office, Dot still had several calls on hold.

Suddenly the most handsome creature she had ever seen strode into the office. "Bye-bye. Gotta go," she said to the President. She jumped into the arms of the visitor, who happened to be Mel Gibson. "Hellooo, Nurse!" said Dot.

"I'd like to see Mr. Plotz," Mel Gibson told her.

Dot batted her eyelashes. "Do you believe in love at first leap?" she said.

"I need to see Mr. Plotz," he repeated.

"Why don't we talk about us?" said Dot.

"Why don't I wait?" said Mr. Gibson. He tried to pull Dot off him as politely as he could. She stuck like glue.

"Let's stay like this forever," Dot said.

Mel yanked himself free. "Isn't he adorable?" sighed Dot.

He settled himself on a couch to wait
for Mr. Plotz. Dot suddenly appeared in an
evening gown. "Didn't I meet you on a
summer cruise ship?" she asked.

"I . . . I've never been on a summer
cruise ship," stuttered Mel.

"Well, this is your lucky day!" yelled
Dot. She threw confetti into the air. "I just
happen to have two tickets for a romantic
cruise to Bora Bora!"

Mel Gibson was horrified. "On second
thought . . . I'll just call," he said as he fled
from the office.

Meanwhile, in Mr. Plotz's office, Yakko
was still handing Mr. Plotz papers to sign.
"Here," Yakko said, pointing to a spot on a
paper. "Here. Here."

Yakko pointed to Mr. Plotz's face. Mr. Plotz was so busy signing he signed his own forehead! He signed both cheeks, his nose, and his chin before he noticed he was covered with ink. He wiped his face and glared at Yakko.

"Sorry, your chairmanship. I got carried away," said Yakko. Mr. Plotz tossed him out of the office.

Yakko landed on a pile of papers and began to read. Suddenly he remembered one of the papers was a check. "Weeeeee're rich!" he shouted. He hugged himself and kissed the check. Mr. Plotz stormed out of his office, grabbed the check out of Yakko's hand, and slammed the door.

"Weeeeee're poor!" Yakko cried.

Later that day Yakko, Wakko, and Dot stood at attention as Mr. Plotz spouted out orders. "Wakko, I want you to make copies! Yakko, type this memo! Dot, file these papers!"

The Animaniacs nodded and smiled sweetly, but they didn't move. "Well, get to work!" screamed Mr. Plotz, and headed back into his office.

Yakko, Wakko, and Dot launched into high gear. Yakko cracked his knuckles and began to type at a feverish pace. *Clickety clack, clickety clack*! So what if he didn't have a typewriter!

Dot picked up a file folder, took a nail file out of the drawer, and began to file it across the folder. *Scratch, scratch, scratch* went the nail file. Soon there was nothing left of the file folder. The air was filled with paper dust.

Meanwhile, Wakko was busy copying. He opened the lid of the copy machine, stuck his face in, and pressed the button. After a moment a paper came out with a picture of Wakko's very silly face on it. "Perfect," he said. "Looks just like me."

Now he began to make copies of every part of himself. Faster and faster the copies came. Wakko couldn't figure out how to shut off the machine. Finally, he picked up a mallet and wacked it. The machine sputtered to a stop.

"I'm done," called out Yakko. He pulled
a real piece of paper out of the imaginary
typewriter.

"I'm done," said Dot, sitting in a pile of
paper file shavings.

"Me, too!" said Wakko, from under a
huge pile of paper.

Just then the telephone rang.

"Helloooo, Nurse! Please hold," said Yakko, grabbing the receiver at the last second.

Wakko clenched his fists. "I never get to get it," he said, his face red with anger.

Wakko's body trembled. His eyes spun in his head. He looked as if he might explode. Then Mr. Plotz called him.

"Wakko," Mr. Plotz said. "I need you in my office."

Wakko stopped trembling. He unclenched his fists and his face returned to its normal shape. He held his head high and strutted into the boss's office.

"Sit down," Mr. Plotz said, once Wakko was in his office. Wakko nodded and immediately sat down in Mr. Plotz's chair. It was at least four times bigger than Wakko but he sat up straight and tall. He was proud to be of service.

"I want you to take a letter," Mr. Plotz said, pacing back and forth.

"Where do you want me to take it?" Wakko asked.

"No. No. I mean, I want you to write a letter," Mr. Plotz said in frustration.

"Oh. Okay," Yakko replied. He grabbed a pen and began the letter. *"Dear Santa,"* he said as he wrote. *"I have been ever so good this year. I would like a new mallet and a shiny brass anvil."*

"No! No! No!" Mr. Plotz shouted. "Write a letter for ME!"

Wakko looked a bit confused. "I don't know what you want for Christmas," he replied.

With that Mr. Plotz picked up Wakko and sent him flying into the outer office. Wakko landed on Dot's desk.

"Dot! Get in here!" called Mr. Plotz. "I need to dictate a letter."

"Just a moment," Dot answered. She stuck a pencil in Wakko's mouth and cranked his ear as if he were a pencil sharpener. His eyes spun around in his head. Dot took the sharpened pencil and scampered into Mr. Plotz's office.

A few moments later Dot was seated across from Mr. Plotz. She was scribbling furiously on a pad of paper.

"In conclusion, it is imperative . . . ," Mr. Plotz droned on, " . . . that this movie be brought in under budget and on time. Sincerely, Thaddeus Plotz." The big boss hovered over Dot. "Dot, read that back to me," he ordered.

"Read what back to you?" asked Dot.

"The letter I just dictated!" yelled Mr. Plotz.

"What letter?" Dot asked. "I'm sorry, were you saying something?"

Grabbing the pad out of her hand Mr. Plotz looked at what she had written. There were only three words on the page: *Dot and Mel*. Underneath them was a big heart with a picture of Dot and Mel Gibson holding hands!

"Oooooh!" Mr. Plotz was ready to burst. He called Yakko into his office.

"Yakko? Can you take dictation?" Mr. Plotz asked.

"Of course!" Yakko assured him.

Thrusting the pen and paper into Yakko's hands, Mr. Plotz heaved a sigh of relief. "Finally!" he said.

"Where do you want me to take it?" Yakko asked.

Mr. Plotz's face twitched and turned red. His eyes grew bloodshot. "*Aaaaaahhhhhhhh!*" he screamed, his voice shaking the whole building.

"Take it easy, Thad," Yakko said as Mr. Plotz came nearer and nearer.

Suddenly the door burst open and in ran Wakko and Dot. "Who screamed?" asked Dot.

"He did," said Yakko, pointing to Mr. Plotz. "He just blew."

"Get out of my life!" screamed Mr. Plotz.

But before he could throw the Animaniacs out of his office, the telephone rang.

"I'll get it!" cried Yakko, Wakko, and Dot.

But this time Wakko was determined to get there first. He beat Yakko and Dot to the door, slammed it behind him, and pulled a steel gate across it. Then a steel door, then an elevator door! At top speed, he covered it all with a layer of bricks and mortar.

25

Inside Mr. Plotz's office, Yakko and Dot
were trying to open the door, but it
wouldn't budge. Yakko whipped out a
can of paint and drew a door on the wall.

As soon as he finished, he and Dot raced through the painted door to the outer office.

Wakko was just picking up the phone when Yakko and Dot arrived on the scene. The three of them began to wrestle. They wrestled themselves into a giant cloud of dust. But Dot tiptoed out of the dust cloud, carrying the telephone.

Next Yakko poked his head out of the cloud, grabbed hold of the cord, and yanked the phone from Dot's hands. It flew through the air and landed in Yakko's arms. As he was about to answer it, Wakko snatched it and raced out of the room.

The phone cord stretched further and further as Wakko ran. Soon the cord was pulling telephone poles against the building.

Wakko sped along smiling as Dot raced by and plucked the phone from his arms. But Wakko was too quick for her and grabbed it away.

Back in his office, Mr. Plotz wondered what was going on. He opened the painted door. In ran Wakko, carrying the phone like a football. Yakko and Dot followed close behind.

Running in circles, the three crazy Animaniacs soon had the desk, office, and Mr. Plotz tangled in the cord.

"Stop!" screamed Mr. Plotz.

"Time out!" shouted Yakko. They all froze in their tracks.

Mr. Plotz was boiling. "When will this insanity end?"

"When one of us answers the phone, silly," Dot replied, as though it were completely obvious.

"I didn't know that," said Mr. Plotz, scratching his head.

"Time in!" Yakko shouted suddenly.

The Animaniacs went back to racing around the room. Yakko and Dot chased Wakko up and down the walls and across the ceiling. Wakko was having the time of his life.

By now the cord was pulled so tightly that the telephone poles almost came through the windows. Suddenly the weight of the poles was too much. *Crash! Bang!* The walls collapsed into a pile of rubble. The only thing left standing was a brick archway.

Ring . . . Ring!

Yakko, Wakko, and Dot poked their heads out of the rubble.

30

Wakko felt around beneath him and daintily pulled out the phone. "I'll get it," he cried happily. "Hello? Uh. Uh. Uh. Okay. Buh-bye."

"That was your secretary," Wakko said, turning to Mr. Plotz. "She's still sick. You get us for one more day."

Mr. Plotz looked out from the ruins of his office. For a moment, he looked as if he were going to faint. Then, a brick broke free of the arch and clonked him on the head. *Thump!* He *did* faint.

"La La Law"

It was a beautiful, bright sunny day in Burbank, California. Dr. Scratchansniff, the famous psychologist, had a number of errands to do and this was the perfect day to do them.

Best of all, the Burbank Psychoanalyst Shoppe was having its annual 50% Off Sale. He parked his car and hurried inside. Within seconds, he had spotted just what he wanted: an Acme Psychiatry Couch. He paid for it and lugged the crate outside.

When he got to his car he noticed a pink slip of paper on the windshield. It read: *Parking Ticket — City of Burbank — Have a nice day.*

"A parking ticket," he said, angrily snatching up the paper. "But why? I put money in the meter." How could he possibly have a nice day now?

Back in his office, Dr. Scratchansniff showed the ticket to the Animaniacs — Yakko, Wakko, and Dot.

"If you're innocent, then you've got to *fight* this ticket!" said Yakko.

"We'll even help you!" Wakko added.

"We'll be your lawyers!" Dot volunteered.

Dr. Scratchansniff burst out laughing. "You? My lawyers! Oh, no no no!

"You kids are crazy," he said, turning serious. He grabbed the ticket from Yakko. "I'm going to pay the ticket and that's that." Dr. Scratchansniff walked out the door.

A second later Dr. Scratchansniff was back. "And don't come anywhere near me!" With that he slammed the door.

That was too much for the Animaniacs to resist. Now they knew the good doctor *really* needed their help!

"Come, siblings, we have a trial to prepare," Yakko said to Wakko and Dot.

The three of them twirled into a blur. When they came to a stop they were dressed in suits and carried briefcases. They looked just like TV lawyers.

The next day, Dr. Scratchansniff stood meekly in a courtroom in the Burbank Hall of Justice.

"Dr. Otto Scratchansniff?" the judge called. He peered down at Scratchansniff. "You're charged with a parking violation. You can pay the ticket or try to prove your innocence."

Dr. Scratchansniff reached into his pocket. "I brought my checkbook so I'll just—"

"Fight!" a loud voice interrupted.

"Oh, no! Not *them*!" Dr. Scratchansniff said in horror.

"Who said that?" asked the judge, looking around the courtroom.

34

Suddenly Yakko's head popped out of a water pitcher on the judge's bench. "I did, your judgity!" he cried and gave the judge a big kiss on the head.

"What is the meaning of this?" roared the judge, shaking his finger in Yakko's face.

"That's a finger," Yakko replied. "You have five of them on each hand — unless you're in the circus. Then it's negotiable."

Yakko pulled himself all the way out of the pitcher and stood on the bench. "Allow me to introduce my associates." He laid his briefcase on the bench and opened it.

Out popped Wakko and Dot, each giving him a big smooch on the head.

"I don't know who you think you are, but this is highly irregular!" said the judge.

"We're Dr. Scratchansniff's lawyers," Dot answered.

"Please, please go away," begged Dr. Scratchansniff.

Yakko took Dr. Scratchansniff by the hand and dragged him to the defense table. "You just sit right down here and leave everything to us," Yakko said.

"Help," Dr. Scratchansniff pleaded in a tiny voice.

Dot was standing off to one side. Her frame cast a long shadow on the ground. Yakko walked over and joined her.

"Mr. Judgeperson, we'll prove that Dr. Scratchansniff is innocent ... beyond a shadow of a Dot," Yakko said, glancing at the shadow.

"I hate puns," the judge said as he tried to ignore Yakko's bad joke.

"We will also prove ..." Yakko continued as Dot and Wakko dragged a blindfolded statue into the room, "... that justice is not blind. She's cross-eyed."

He whipped the blindfold off the statue. The statue's eyes were badly crossed. Yakko handed the statue a pair of glasses. Her marble face cracked a smile.

"Now see here!" the judge yelled. "I've had just about enough of this folderol!"

With that the Animaniacs all stood together and began to sing. "Falderee! Falderaa! Haa! Haa! Haa!"

Bang! Bang! Bang! The judge pounded his gavel on the bench. "Can we just get on with the trial? Do you have any witnesses?" he asked.

"Yes," Yakko said.

"Then call your first witness!" the judge screamed.

"May I please say something?" Dr. Scratchansniff interrupted.

"No!" the Animaniacs answered all together as they pulled him back down into his seat.

"Your immensity, we call to the stand the person who gave Dr. Scratchansniff the ticket: Burbank Meter Maid, Miss Gerty Bilchmoyntner."

A door in the back of the courtroom burst open and a little three-wheeled police cart entered. The vehicle drove to the front of the courtroom and out stepped a woman dressed in a hideous meter maid suit. It was Miss Gerty Bilchmoyntner.

39

Miss Bilchmoyntner stepped into the witness stand and prepared to testify. She raised her hand in the air.

"Do you swear?" Wakko asked.

"Yes," Miss Bilchmoyntner answered.

"Well, you shouldn't," Yakko scolded her. "It's not nice." He walked away in disgust.

"You may be seated now, Miss Bilchmoyntner," said the judge.

Once Miss Bilchmoyntner had taken her seat on the witness stand, Dot approached her and leaned in close. Her face was only an inch from Miss Bilchmoyntner's.

"Miss Bilchmoyntner ...," Dot said in a drippingly sweet tone of voice. She consulted the clipboard she carried. Suddenly her voice grew angry. "Or isn't your real name Nana Puntridge of Palo Alto, California?"

"No," replied Miss Bilchmoyntner.

"Oh," said Dot, completely disappointed. Throwing the clipboard away, Dot quickly returned to her seat. "I'm done," she said.

Throughout all this, Dr. Scratchansniff sat with his head in his hands. He was trying to pretend that he had never even seen the Animaniacs before.

Now it was Wakko's turn to question the witness. Yakko patted Wakko on the back as he approached the stand. "Go for it," Yakko advised his younger brother.

Wakko walked purposefully to the witness stand, gripped the edge of it, pointed to Miss Bilchmoyntner, opened his mouth, and said ... nothing.

He placed his hand on his chin and began to think. He started to pace back and forth. Suddenly he had an idea. He raced to the stand, pointed at Miss Bilchmoyntner, opened his mouth, and said ... nothing.

Wakko went back to pacing, hands behind his back. All at once he stopped, whirled to face the stand, and prepared to speak. But again nothing came out.

The judge had had enough. "Will you get on with it!" he screamed.

Now Wakko looked directly at Miss Bilchmoyntner. "Miss Bilchmoyntner! Do you . . ." he began in a loud voice, ". . . like candy?" he finished with a smile.

"Yes," Miss Bilchmoyntner answered.

"Do you have any?" Wakko asked hopefully.

"No," Miss Bilchmoyntner replied.

"I'm through," Wakko said, clearly disappointed. He walked back to his seat beside Yakko. "Your turn," he told his brother.

But Yakko was now in a bad mood. All of the good questions had been asked and no important new information had come out. "Oh, thank you," he said sarcastically. "I have so much to go on."

Yakko decided to take the direct approach.

"Miss Bilchmoyntner," he said, pointing to Dr. Scratchansniff. "Why did you give Dr. Scratchansniff a ticket?"

"His parking meter had expired. That's against the law," the meter maid replied.

Yakko began to pace around the room. "Miss Bilchmoyntner, you're a meter maid, is that correct?"

"Yes," Miss Bilchmoyntner said.

"Do you do windows?" Yakko asked.

"Of course not!" Miss Bilchmoyntner exclaimed.

"Then what kind of maid are you?" Yakko asked angrily.

"Stop badgering the witness," the judge barked.

Yakko pulled away the big, furry badger he was holding in Miss Bilchmoyntner's face and set the animal aside.

"You kids are driving me crazy!" the judge roared.

Dr. Scratchansniff still sat with his head in his hands. "I wonder what prison is like," he moaned.

Yakko, who was not in the least disturbed — at least not by the situation in the courtroom — picked up where he had left off. "Now, Miss Bilchmoyntner," he began. "Is it not possible that because you're such a terrible maid, the meter might have been dirty and malfunctioning?"

"Well, I suppose anything's possible," Miss Bilchmoyntner replied, still a bit confused by Yakko's odd questions. "But ..."

Yakko pressed on. "And isn't that what happened? You gave him a ticket he didn't deserve!"

"Stop leading the witness," the judge ordered.

By now Yakko and Miss Bilchmoyntner were dancing cheek to cheek in a tango. "All right then, *you* lead," Yakko told Miss Bilchmoyntner, forcing her to lead the dance.

By now, Yakko and Miss Bilchmoyntner were having a blast. "Everybody!" Yakko shouted, inviting the others to join in.

At Yakko's command, Dot grabbed the judge and they danced around the room. Then Wakko began to tango with Dr. Scratchansniff. Back and forth the three sets of dance partners tangoed.

"Switch!" called Yakko.

Suddenly everyone changed partners. Now Yakko and Wakko danced together. Dot paired up with Dr. Scratchansniff. And the judge and Miss Bilchmoyntner teamed up.

"I love to tango," the judge said, holding Miss Bilchmoyntner in his arms.

"Oh, judge," Miss Bilchmoyntner giggled. "But what about the trial?"

"Forget about the trial. Let's talk about *us*," the judge said romantically.

As the judge and Miss Bilchmoyntner tangoed down the aisle to the back of the courtroom, the doors opened. The Animaniacs stood on either side of the aisle, throwing rice as if it were a wedding.

"Case dismissed," said the judge as he and Miss Bilchmoyntner tangoed out of the courtroom.